The exciting adventure story of Diarmaid and Gráinne who anger Fionn, the fierce warrior leader of the Fianna, by running away together. Fionn pursues them across Ireland using his skill as a fighter and his magic powers to try to overcome them. Luckily, Diarmaid has a foster-father who is a druid and who can help him too. But Fionn finally catches up with him ... Third in the series of classic Celtic tales from Liam Mac Uistin.

What they said about THE TÁIN
'An exciting story, highly recommended'
Wicklow People

What they said about CELTIC MAGIC TALES
'This book really is magical!'
Evening Herald

The Hunt for

ÓiARMAiÒ
AnÒ
GRÁinne

Liam Mac Uistin

Illustrated by Laura Cronin

THE O'BRIEN PRESS
DUBLIN

First published 1996 by The O'Brien Press Ltd.,
20 Victoria Road, Rathgar, Dublin 6, Ireland.

ISBN 0-86278-480-8

British Library Cataloguing-in-Publication Data
Mac Uistin, Liam
The Hunt for Diarmaid and Gráinne
1. Children's stories, English
I.Title II. Cronin, Laura
823.9'14 [J]

1 2 3 4 5 6 7 8 9 10
96 97 98 99 00 01 02 03

The O'Brien Press Ltd receives assistance from
The Arts Council/An Chomhairle Ealaíon

Typesetting, editing, layout, design: The O'Brien Press Ltd.
Cover illustration: Laura Cronin
Cover separations: Irish Photo Ltd., Dublin
Printing: Cox & Wyman Ltd., Reading

Contents

Prologue PAGE 9

CHAPTER ONE PAGE 13
Fionn Mac Cumhaill is Lonely

CHAPTER TWO PAGE 18
A Most Unusual Wedding Feast

CHAPTER THREE PAGE 28
The Hunt Begins

CHAPTER FOUR PAGE 36
Aongus to the Rescue

CHAPTER FIVE PAGE 40
The Warning

CHAPTER SIX PAGE 46
The Magic Quicken Tree

CHAPTER SEVEN PAGE 53
Trapped in the Tree

CHAPTER EIGHT PAGE 58
The Escape

CHAPTER NINE PAGE 63
Peace

CHAPTER TEN PAGE 66
The *Geis*

CHAPTER ELEVEN PAGE 72
The Treachery of Fionn Mac Cumhaill

For Ailish, with love

The Hunt for
Diarmaid and Gráinne

PROLOGUE

The story of 'The Hunt for Diarmaid and Gráinne' comes from the enchanting store of legendary lore that is part of the Celtic tradition in Ireland. It belongs to the *Fiannaíocht*, the colourful cycle of story and poetry about the exploits of the great warrior Fionn Mac Cumhaill, who in olden times led an heroic band of soldiers known as the Fianna. *'Tóraíocht Dhiarmada agus Ghráinne'* or 'The Hunt for Diarmaid and Gráinne' is the most exciting and romantic of all the tales in the *Fiannaíocht*. It is a poignant story of love, bravery and betrayal. This account tracks Diarmaid and Gráinne as they flee from the burning vengeance of Fionn, and is one of the sources of the world-famous story of Tristan and Isolde, the doomed lovers who fled the vengeance of a king.

Like most of the old Celtic tales this story was probably first passed on by word of mouth. Later, it appeared in different written versions. The earliest surviving copy of one of these manuscripts dates from the middle of the sixteenth century.

The tale also shows us the world of that colourful band of warriors known as the Fianna. These fearless men – and they were always men! – made up a standing army whose main duty was to guard the shores of Ireland from foreign invaders. In order to be accepted into the Fianna a warrior had to undergo several very severe tests. First, he had to stand in a hole in the ground, which meant he could not move from his knees down. Then with only a hazel staff and a shield to defend himself, he fought against nine men armed with spears. If any of the spears thrown at him drew even one drop of blood he was not taken into the Fianna.

Next, he was hunted through the woods by the other warriors. If he was wounded or caught or if his spear shook in his hand while he was defending himself; or if he let a single strand of his hair be caught in a tree branch, he was not accepted. If, while fleeing from his pursuers, he stood on a thorn, he had to pluck it out without stopping. He also had to make sure that he ran so lightly that no dry twig broke under his foot.

While in flight, he had to leap over branches as high as his head and stoop under others as low as his knee without leaving a trembling leaf or branch behind. If he succeeded in passing all these tests of strength and agility, the warrior had then to be able to recite the *Twelve Books of Poetry* and know all the ancient tales and legends of Ireland.

Finally, if he fulfilled all these difficult requirements he was accepted into the Fianna. He took four vows of chivalry which bound him never to ask for a dowry with a wife, never to take cattle that belonged to another man, never to refuse help to anyone seeking it, and never to give way in combat to less than nine warriors.

In peace-time there were three *cathas* or battalions of

the Fianna, with three thousand men in each *catha*; in war-time this increased to seven *cathas*. Twenty-one thousand brave men trained in spear-throwing, running, hunting and great feats of arms made a very formidable force.

The Fianna were great hunters as well as warriors. From May to November they lived in the open, sleeping in rough huts or under the stars. They moved from place to place, hunting in the woods, fishing in the rivers and lakes and guarding the shores of the island against invaders.

They ate only one meal a day which they prepared when they were encamped in the evening. They dug pits in the ground in which they built great fires. Once the flames were leaping, they threw in large stones to heat. They laid the fresh meat of the animals they had killed that day, wrapped in green rushes, on the stones and waited for it to cook. After eating, they sat around the roaring fire and listened to the stories and poems of the bards or *filí*. They slept then on beds made of green boughs covered by moss and rushes.

At the time of Diarmaid and Gráinne the role of the Fianna was to defend Ireland and to uphold the authority of the High King, Cormac Mac Airt. However they took an oath of loyalty not to the king but to their leader, Fionn Mac Cumhaill.

High King Cormac gave Fionn the great fort of Allen as his headquarters. This stood on the Hill of Allen in Kildare and was a very grand place indeed with its massive walls, splendid hall, chariot houses and warriors' sleeping places.

Fionn Mac Cumhaill was an ideal leader, tall, brave and kind. If he had to give judgement in a dispute between a stranger and a friend he would be as fair to the stranger as to his friend. But it was said of him that he also had a dark side to his nature, a harsh bitter side, and he never forgave anyone who did him a wrong.

And, as we shall see, it is the dark side of Fionn Mac Cumhaill that emerges in this story …

CHAPTER ONE

Fionn Mac Cumhaill is Lonely

Fionn Mac Cumhaill was not happy. He stood at the window in the great hall of his fort on the Hill of Allen and stared down discontentedly at the River Liffey as it rolled across the plain of Kildare and on towards the sea.

Two swans came into view, their necks touching. A pang of loneliness gripped him. Unlike the swans he had no partner to bring love and warmth into his life. Since the death of his second wife, Manissa, he had had no woman at his side.

He turned away from the window and caught a glimpse of himself in the mirror of burnished brass that hung upon the wall. The furrow of discontent on his brow grew deeper. He was growing old. The fair hair which gave him his name was turning grey and his tall sturdy frame was becoming stooped. He sighed. Soon he would be seventy.

The door of the great hall swung open and his son Oisín, with Dering, one of his bodyguards, hurried into the room.

'Let's go hunting, Father,' Oisín said. 'There are deer

in the Wood of–' Oisín stopped suddenly. 'Is there something wrong? Are you ill, Father?'

'I am low in spirit,' his father replied. 'Since my beloved Manissa died I have been alone. I long for a wife and companion.'

Oisín nodded sympathetically. He missed Manissa too, although he was the son of Fionn's first wife, Saba.

'You should marry again,' he advised.

'Yes,' said Dering, 'and I know the woman best fitted to be the wife of the great leader of the Fianna.'

Fionn's eyes lit up. 'Who is she?' he asked.

'Gráinne, the daughter of Cormac Mac Airt, High King of Ireland,' replied Dering.

'Of course!' said Oisín. 'I saw her in Tara at the great feast Cormac Mac Airt gave for her twentieth birthday. She is without question the most beautiful woman in Ireland – with long golden hair that falls to her waist, and eyes the colour of the sea under a summer sky. She is the most enchanting woman I know – and the most intelligent. Gráinne would be an ideal wife for you, Father.'

Fionn shook his head dubiously. 'Cormac and I have not been friends since I won his best chariot horse in a game of chess. He would undoubtedly refuse me permission to marry his daughter.'

'Let me go to Tara and ask the High King on your behalf,' Oisín said.

'Very well,' said Fionn. 'And as a token of my goodwill, you may take him back his chariot horse.'

Fionn watched from the window as Oisín ordered one

of the horse boys to make his chariot ready. He saw Oisín
set off, urging his horses on till they outpaced the wind,
on the forty-eight kilometre journey to the High King's
palace on the Hill of Tara in Meath. Cormac's beautiful
chariot horse ran alongside him. When his son's chariot
disappeared from sight Fionn turned away from the
window and sighed. He knew Oisín was a diplomat as
well as a warrior, but Fionn doubted that the mission
would be a success.

The towers and walls of the High King's palace
shimmered in the blazing sun, as Oisín drew near.
He leapt from his chariot and hurried into the garden
where Cormac Mac Airt was playing a game of chess with
his *seanachie* or royal historian. When Cormac saw
Oisín's dusty clothes he nodded to the *seanachie* to
withdraw into the palace.

'What brings you to Tara, Oisín?' he asked coldly. 'It
has been many months since we last met.'

'My father wishes to repair the rift between you,' Oisín
replied. 'As a token of his goodwill he is returning the
chariot horse he won from you.'

A smile flickered across the High King's face. This
was good news! He had no wish to prolong the feud
with Fionn. Although he had his own army at Tara, a
clash with the Fianna – a devoted warrior army who
would fight to the death – was still to be avoided at all
costs. Besides, he had always enjoyed Fionn's com-
pany at the royal feasts in the palace and at the chess

table, even if he did win too often.

'I would be glad to renew our friendship,' he said.

Oisín was relieved. 'My father also wishes to marry again,' he said. 'He would be honoured if your daughter, the lovely Princess Gráinne, would agree to be his wife.'

Cormac stroked his rich red beard doubtfully. 'Hmm. There is hardly a prince in the land who has not sought Gráinne's hand in marriage. But she has refused them all. She is a strong-willed woman and there is little I can do to persuade her to marry even so great a warrior as Fionn. However, I shall ask her so that your father will know I do not harbour any ill-feeling against him.'

The High King brought Oisín to the *grianán* or summer-house which he had built specially for his daughter. There they found Gráinne playing her harp. Oisín gazed at her with undisguised admiration. She had grown even more beautiful since he had last seen her. She rose to her feet and greeted Oisín warmly. They had been friends since she was a child.

'Oisín has come with a marriage proposal on behalf of a very important person,' the High King said.

'Not another one!' snorted Gráinne petulantly. 'I am sick and tired of these silly men bothering me. I have no wish to marry at present.'

'But, Gráinne,' said her father. 'This is no ordinary man. It is the great hero, Fionn Mac Cumhaill, who wishes to marry you.'

Gráinne glanced from her father to Oisín. 'Your father?' she murmured. 'He wants to marry me?'

Oisín nodded, expecting another outburst. Instead,

Gráinne smiled. She had admired Fionn from the m
when, as a child, she had first seen him at one of .
father's feasts in the palace. She had thought him the
finest man she had ever seen and hoped that someday
she would meet a hero like him who would ask her to
be his wife. But no man like that had yet come into her
life.

'I have not seen your father for some years,' she said
to Oisín. 'Is he still as handsome as ever?'

'Yes,' Oisín replied, biting his lip. Old, he thought to
himself, but handsome in his way.

'Then I shall be happy to have him as my husband,'
Gráinne declared.

Cormac heaved a sigh of relief. 'That's settled then,'
he said. 'Oisín, give your father my congratulations and
tell him the wedding will take place here in the palace
in three weeks' time.' He turned to Gráinne. 'I assume
those arrangements suit you, my dear?'

Gráinne nodded in agreement. Oisín thanked them
both and with a light heart set out for his father's fort.
Behind him, carrying on the clear summer air, he could
hear Gráinne's sweet voice, singing to the accompani-
ment of her harp.

'Truly, my father is a fortunate man,' he murmured.

CHAPTER TWO

An Unusual Wedding Feast

Fionn Mac Cumhaill beamed with delight when Oisín told him the good news. His smile grew even broader when Oisín told him of Gráinne's obvious affection for him and of how she had chosen him above all the young princes who had come seeking her hand. He straightened his shoulders and glanced again in the mirror. Despite his age he was still a fine-looking man, he assured himself, and a worthy partner for any beautiful young princess.

He set about preparing for the wedding. He ordered a new tunic of the finest cloth from the best tailor in the land. He told his armourer to shine up his ceremonial sword and dagger and to burnish the splendid gold torc he wore around his neck on ceremonial occasions. And then he waited impatiently as the weeks crawled by.

Finally the wedding day came. Accompanied by his chief warriors, Fionn set out for the palace of Tara. The wedding party presented a magnificent sight as they drove along the road in their gilded chariots, their burnished torcs, armlets and weapons sparkling in the sun, their cloaks of fine cloth billowing behind them in the breeze.

From atop the palace walls of Tara, the fine procession could be seen for many miles and a shrill blast of trumpets greeted the warriors as they arrived. The huge gates were thrown open.

'A hundred thousand welcomes!' cried Cormac Mac Airt as he led them into the palace. He was resplendent in a crimson cloak, clasped at his chest by a brooch studded with precious stones. Around his neck he wore a golden torc, and on his feet were shoes of gold-embroidered cloth. He led his guests in proudly to the *Mí-Cuarta*, the great banqueting hall of Tara. There everyone was seated at a long table according to rank, and each warrior had a place under his own shield which hung upon the wall.

The High King sat at the head of the table on which a magnificent feast was already arrayed. Fionn Mac Cumhaill sat at his right hand, while the seat at his left hand was reserved for the Princess Gráinne who had yet to arrive. On each side of them were seated the kings of Leinster, Munster, Connaught and Ulster and then the chief warriors of the Fianna.

A hush fell on the hall. The Princess Gráinne stood at the doorway. Every man there gazed in fascination at her. She was wearing a gown of the finest silk, caught at the waist by a girdle of gleaming gold. A thin coronet of gold, set with great shining gems of blood red, emerald and azure rested on the crown of her head. A gasp of admiration escaped from Fionn's lips. Oisín was right, Gráinne was the loveliest woman in all of Ireland.

Gráinne took her seat beside the High King and glanced around the table at the guests. Many of them she knew already, but there were some she did not. She smiled at Oisín who was sitting across the table from her and he bowed to her in return. Her gaze rested thoughtfully on the handsome young man, wearing a black headband, who sat beside Oisín. Clearly, he was an important member of the Fianna, but she had no recollection of ever meeting him before. He smiled across the table at her, and her heart gave a leap – how handsome he was.

Other warriors she recognised. That savage-looking man with the one eye was Goll Mac Morna, fierce as a wild boar in battle. The fat man sitting beside him was Conan Maol. He held his place in the Fianna because he was a great fighter and because of his great commonsense and ability to give good advice. Next to him was Dering, of whom it was said that he could tell the future by closing his eyes and contemplating the darkness at the back of his head. And next to him again was Oscar, son of Oisín and one of the bravest warriors in the Fianna.

But where was Fionn Mac Cumhaill, the bravest and most handsome of them all, the hero she had adored ever since she was a little girl?

She gazed around the table again but could not see the tall, fair-haired leader of the Fianna anywhere.

Puzzled, she turned to her father. 'Has Fionn not come yet?' she enquired.

Her father smiled. 'He is here, beside me,' he said.

Gráinne craned her neck to get a good look at the man sitting at the right hand of the High King. He was tall but his hair was turning grey and his face was lined and wrinkled. Surely, this old man was not Fionn Mac Cumhaill, her husband to be? 'Are you sure?' she asked her father.

'Of course I am, daughter,' he replied. 'Why? Don't you recognise him?'

Gráinne shook her head sadly. 'It is some years since I last saw him,' she said quietly. 'He has changed. I did not realise he was so old.'

Her father laughed. 'We all change with the passage of time … even young and beautiful women.'

As the feasting proceeded, and the harpers and singers and jugglers entertained the gathering, Gráinne sat silently contemplating her future. She had no wish now to marry this aged man called Fionn Mac Cumhaill. She should never have agreed to marry him. But she had given her word and to change her mind now would be an insult to the great Fionn and would cause another rift between him and her father. Nor could she involve her dear father in a war which could cost him his life and destroy Tara.

Gráinne sighed. She would have to go ahead with the marriage. She thought wryly of all those fine young men whose offers of marriage she had rejected. Some of them

were almost as handsome as that brown-haired warrior sitting beside Oisín.

She turned and smiled at the man who sat by her side. 'Who is that warrior with the black headband sitting beside Oisín?' she asked.

'That is Diarmaid Ó Duibhne, a brave hero and great friend of Fionn Mac Cumhaill,' the man replied. 'He is sometimes called "Diarmaid of the Women",' he added, 'because of the number of women who have fallen in love with him. He wears that headband to hide the *ball seirce*, the magic love mole, he bears on his forehead. Any woman who sees that mole cannot help falling in love with him for the rest of her life.'

A loud burst of laughter drew her gaze back to the other side of the table where Oisín and Diarmaid were sharing a joke. Diarmaid put his hand to his head and rocked with laughter. As he did so, he accidentally moved the headband and revealed the *ball seirce* on his forehead. Gráinne stared and stared at the magic mole. From that moment her heart was Diarmaid's for life.

Oisín noticed Gráinne gazing in fascination at Diarmaid. Alarmed, he glanced at his companion and saw that the *ball seirce* was showing.

'Quick, Diarmaid, your headband!' he hissed. 'Pull it down! The mole on your forehead is showing.'

Diarmaid immediately pulled the headband back into position, and Oisín glanced anxiously at Gráinne again. She was deep in conversation with her father. Perhaps no harm had been done after all ...

But Gráinne was firmly under the love spell and her mind was concentrated now on how to escape from the hall with Diarmaid. All her previous intentions to go ahead with the marriage to Fionn were forgotten. All she could think about now was how to get Diarmaid to run away with her. She realised that it would not be easy. Her father would try to stop her, and if he did not succeed, Fionn and his warriors certainly would. She must think of some way to make them powerless. A broad smile came over her face. She had decided what to do.

'I am glad to see you so happy, my dear,' her father said. He took up his goblet of wine. 'It is time for me to propose a toast to Fionn and yourself.'

'Not yet, Father,' Gráinne said. 'First, I want you and all our guests to drink from my own drinking-cup.'

She called one of her servants and ordered her to bring the golden drinking-cup she kept in her summer-house. She rose to take the cup, and shielding what she was doing behind the long sleeve of her gown, she tipped open a large ring on her finger. Out of it she poured a turquoise powder into the empty vessel. Then she filled the cup up to the top with wine.

'Pass the cup around to everyone at the table except Diarmaid Ó Duibhne. Tell them I wish them to drink my health from it,' she instructed her servant.

The cup was taken around to all the guests except

Diarmaid. Soon, the clamour of voices and laughter began to grow silent. The guests' heads sank drowsily onto their chests, and one by one they fell into a deep sleep.

Fionn had taken only a sip from the cup when he saw the High King and all the guests, apart from Diarmaid, yawning and sinking sleepily down onto the table. He blinked, trying to stop his eyelids from closing, and stared at Gráinne who smiled back at him in a strange manner. He saw Diarmaid was also gazing around the table in surprise. Then he made a huge effort to rise to his feet, but it was no use – a great wave of drowsiness swept over him and he too slumped in sleep onto the table.

Gráinne rose from her seat and sat beside Diarmaid. 'What is happening?' he said, his face full of alarm. 'Why has everyone except us suddenly fallen asleep?'

'I have arranged this,' Gráinne said, 'because I am in love with you, Diarmaid Ó Duibhne. Will you give me your love too?'

Diarmaid shook his head. 'I cannot,' he declared. 'Any woman who is promised to Fionn Mac Cumhaill can never be mine.'

'But I have no wish to marry that sad old creature!' Gráinne said firmly. 'You are the only man I shall ever love.'

Diarmaid replied, just as firmly, 'Fionn is my friend and leader. I will not betray him.'

'Come away with me now, Diarmaid!' urged Gráinne. 'We will find some place where we can live happily together and neither Fionn nor anyone else will ever find us.'

'There is no place in Ireland where we could hide from the terrible anger of Fionn,' Diarmaid replied. 'Nor do I love you, Gráinne.'

'I will make you love me,' Gráinne said. 'I shall make you very happy if you come away with me now.'

'No!' Diarmaid declared in a firm voice. 'I cannot and I will not.'

'Very well, then,' Gráinne said. 'I will have to try another way. I now put *geas* on you, Diarmaid, a spell that no hero of honour may break. The spell is that you take me with you away from Tara before Fionn or my father or any of the others wake from their sleep.'

'Gráinne, do not do this to me,' Diarmaid pleaded.

'It is already done,' she replied. 'You cannot break the *geas*.'

'But there is no way out,' said Diarmaid. 'The palace doors are locked. They are always locked when your father holds a feast.'

'There is one way,' said Gráinne. 'I have the key to the door from my summer-house to the palace gardens. We can get from there to where the chariots and horses are kept and make our escape before anyone awakes. Come on!'

Diarmaid rose slowly and glanced around at the sleeping figures of Fionn and all his comrades from the Fianna. He felt sad at the thought that he would never hunt with them again or stand shoulder to shoulder with them in battle. But the thing that saddened him most of all was the thought that he was betraying the great leader, Fionn Mac Cumhaill, to whom he had sworn undying loyalty.

With a sigh, Diarmaid followed Gráinne out of the hall.

CHAPTER THREE

The Hunt Begins

Diarmaid and Gráinne slipped out quietly through the door leading from her summer-house into the palace gardens. They paused in the shadow of a hedge and listened for any sounds of alarm from the palace. But all was quiet within. Cautiously, they made their way through the gardens until they came to the place where the horses of the guests were grazing. A magnificent gilded vehicle with two snow-white horses between its shafts stood nearest to them.

'Let us take this one,' Gráinne said.

Diarmaid shook his head. 'No,' he said. 'That one belongs to Fionn Mac Cumhaill. It is bad enough for me to take the woman he was to marry away from him, without stealing his chariot as well.'

He pointed to a smaller chariot with two black horses yoked to it. 'That is mine,' he said, 'And the horses are strong and fleet-footed.'

As they stepped into his chariot, Diarmaid took the reins and they sped away from the palace along the *Slí Mór*, the road that led westwards away from Tara.

Gráinne stood proudly in the chariot, holding Diarmaid's arm, her golden hair streaming out in the wind behind her. She laughed with exhilaration. She was not going to marry Fionn, instead she would spend her life with the one man she truly loved.

But Diarmaid did not share her joy. He wished he had never seen Gráinne. And he feared what would happen if Fionn and the Fianna ever caught up with them. He glanced sideways at Gráinne with her glowing, excited face. Although he did not love her, he was bound by his vows of chivalry to protect her and that he would do even if it meant sacrificing his own life.

When they arrived at the ford across the River Shannon, Diarmaid pulled the horses to a halt.

'We must get out here and continue by foot,' he said.

'Why can't we take the chariot across?' asked Gráinne.

'Because Fionn and his men will follow the horse and wheel tracks,' he replied.

'Won't they follow our footsteps too?'

'Not if we succeed in throwing them off the track.' And with that he took Gráinne in his arms and scrambled into the river to carry her upstream. A mile or so later he clambered back up the river-bank and placed her gently on her feet.

They walked on into the west until they came to a great wood. Deep in the heart of the wood, Diarmaid drew his sword and cut branches from a great oak tree to build a hut with seven doors. He made a soft bed of downy birch for Gráinne to rest on.

'Why have you put all those doors on this hut?' Gráinne asked.

'Just as a precaution,' Diarmaid replied. He tried not to show any anxiety as he spoke, but he knew how ruthless Fionn could be when he felt he had been betrayed.

Back in the palace, Oisín was the first to wake up. When he looked around and saw all the sleeping figures at the table he shook himself. Perhaps he was still dreaming. But soon he realised that this was no dream and that Gráinne had played some strange trick when she gave them her cup to drink from.

She had vanished from her seat opposite him. Oisín turned to wake Diarmaid up and saw that he was gone too. Then, with a sinking feeling, he remembered how the love mole on Diarmaid's forehead had been revealed and how Gráinne had seen it. She must have come under its spell and fallen deeply in love with Diarmaid.

Oisín glanced anxiously across the table at Fionn. His father was beginning to stir. He grunted, sat up and looked around. Then he noticed Oisín.

'What ... what has happened?' he mumbled. 'Why is everyone asleep?' Then he remembered. 'It was that drink Gráinne gave us!'

He glanced down the table. 'Where is she? Oisín, where is she?' Then he noticed Diarmaid's empty seat. 'And where is Diarmaid?'

'They have gone, Father,' Oisín said quietly.

'Gone? Where? Why? Gráinne and I were to be married!' Fionn stumbled to his feet and bellowed angrily: 'I have been betrayed! That traitor Diarmaid has run away with her!'

'He is not at fault, Father,' Oisín said, and he explained how Gráinne had seen the *ball seirce*.

'Even so,' Fionn growled, 'why did Diarmaid agree to go away with her? He was my friend. I trusted him as much as I trust you. How could he commit this act of treachery?'

'Gráinne probably put him under *geasa* to take her away,' said Oisín.

'Then they are both traitors!' snorted Fionn.

The other guests around the table were yawning and rubbing their eyes. Cormac raised his head and opened his mouth to say something to Fionn, but the leader of the Fianna rose and walked away. The High King looked in bewilderment at Oisín who explained what had happened.

The story of Gráinne's elopement with Diarmaid spread like wildfire around the hall. Some of the guests began to smile and snigger in Fionn's direction. That was it. Fionn's anger had been cooling, but now, with his own warriors laughing at him, he became furious.

'I will not rest until I have taken vengeance on those who betrayed me!' he shouted.

A sudden hush fell over the hall. The sniggering stopped. Everyone knew that Fionn Mac Cumhaill was not to be trifled with when his terrible anger was aroused.

Fionn ordered the Fianna to prepare to hunt down Diarmaid and Gráinne. He sent for his trackers, men of the Clann Neamhain who were specially skilled in following the tracks left by fugitives. 'Go immediately,' he ordered, 'and find the tracks of Diarmaid and Gráinne. I shall follow with the Fianna.'

The Clann Neamhain pursued the trail of Diarmaid and Gráinne westwards. When the trackers reached the ford across the Shannon they came to a halt under a large oak tree and waited for Fionn and the Fianna to catch up with them.

'We have lost the trail,' they said to Fionn.

'You had better find it again,' he said grimly, 'or I will hang you from that tree.'

The trackers hurried upstream and picked up the trail again. They followed it swiftly until they reached the hut where Diarmaid and Gráinne were hiding.

'They are in there,' they informed Fionn when he and his warriors reached them.

'Now I shall have my revenge,' Fionn hissed, drawing out his sword. 'Surround the hut!' he ordered.

Oisín glanced anxiously at Dering. Diarmaid was their close friend and they had no wish to see him die.

'We must warn Diarmaid,' Oisín whispered. 'Make the call of a blackbird.' The song of the blackbird was the signal the three friends always used between them when

out hunting and when danger was near. They knew that Diarmaid would recognise it as a warning.

Dering nodded and they imitated the loud song of a blackbird.

'Do you hear that blackbird call?' Diarmaid asked Gráinne inside the hut. 'My friends are warning me that Fionn is outside.'

'We must try and escape!' Gráinne exclaimed.

Diarmaid shook his head. 'The hut is surrounded,' he said. 'I'm afraid we are trapped.'

'Let Fionn kill me then as well as you,' Gráinne said defiantly, 'for I have no wish to live without you.'

Diarmaid looked at her admiringly then. 'You are a brave woman,' he said, and he put his arm around her reassuringly. 'All is not yet lost, Gráinne. I will try to send a thought-message to Aongus, my foster-father. He is of the Tuatha de Danann and may be able to help us with his magic.'

CHAPTER FOUR

Aongus to the Rescue

In a cave in the Boyne Valley Aongus stirred uneasily in his sleep. He woke up and glanced around him, his face clouded with worry. He had a sudden premonition that his foster-son, Diarmaid Ó Duibhne, was in danger.

He rose, went over to the far side of the cave where he practised his magic arts and looked into a magic bowl that rested on a ledge. He ruffled the water in the bowl with his finger. As the water became calmed again it showed a picture that caused Aongus to grow even more worried. His foster-son was indeed in danger – great danger!

Throwing on his magic cloak, Aongus went to the mouth of the cave. He stood there a moment, his long thin arms and hands stretched out like a great bird about to take flight. Then, launching himself into the air, he flew swiftly on the wind and sped westwards from the Boyne until he reached the hut in the wood. Diarmaid and Gráinne stared in amazement when he suddenly appeared in front of them.

'What is the cause of this trouble you are in?' he asked his foster-son.

Diarmaid explained how Gráinne had compelled him to run away with her from the feast at Tara. 'And now Fionn and his warriors have come here seeking revenge,' he concluded.

Aongus sighed. 'Fionn is a formidable enemy.' He spread out his cloak. 'But let the two of you come under my cloak and I will bring you out of here without Fionn or his warriors knowing anything about it.

Diarmaid shook his head. 'Take Gráinne with you,' he said. 'I will stay here and try and make my own way out. If I live, I will follow you. But if I die take Gráinne back to her father for him to deal with as he pleases.'

'No!' Gráinne protested. 'I will not leave you!'

Once more, Diarmaid was impressed by her bravery. 'Go with Aongus,' he said more gently. 'It will be easier for us both.'

Reluctantly, Gráinne slipped under Aongus's cloak and, invisible to Fionn and his warriors, they flew away on the wind. As soon as they were gone Diarmaid grabbed his spears and stood at the nearest door.

'Who is out there?' he called.

'Caoilte Mac Ronáin and his comrades,' came the answer. 'Come out, Diarmaid, and we will protect you.'

'I will not come out for fear that Fionn will blame you for helping me,' Diarmaid said.

He moved on to the next door and asked the same question.

'Conan of the Grey Rushes, together with Clann Morna,' a voice replied. 'Come out to us, Diarmaid, and we will let no one harm you.'

'No,' said Diarmaid. 'Fionn would kill you all if you did that.'

He went to the third door and asked who was outside.

'Goan, a friend of yours,' came the answer. 'Come out here, Diarmaid, and you will be safe.'

'I cannot do that,' said Diarmaid and he moved to the fourth door.

When he asked who was there, a voice said, 'Mac Glóir of the Ulster Fianna. They are here with me now. Come out to us, Diarmaid, and we will make sure you come to no harm.'

'No,' Diarmaid declared, 'for you and your father are my friends and I would not like you to become enemies of Fionn because of me.'

At the fifth door, the answer came: 'Oisín and Oscar and Dering are here, Diarmaid. Come out to us and you will be safe.'

'I will not come out and bring trouble on you,' Diarmaid said. And he went to the sixth door and put his question.

'Clann Neamhain, sworn enemies of yours,' came the answer. 'Come out here, Diarmaid, and we will cut you to pieces!'

'I am not afraid of mean half-shoed trackers like you!' Diarmaid hissed. 'But none of you is worth wasting a weapon on!'

He went to the seventh door and asked who was out there.

'Fionn Mac Cumhaill and the Leinster Fianna,' a voice snarled. 'Come out to us, Diarmaid, and we will carve the flesh from your bones!'

'This is the door I want!' Diarmaid shouted.

He opened the door and rushed out. A row of spears bristled before him, and a triumphant growl came from Fionn's throat. But before any of them could harm him, Diarmaid clutched the shafts of his own spears and, with a mighty spring, soared up in the air, high over Fionn and his warriors.

Then he ran like a deer until he reached the Wood of the Two Swallows where Gráinne and Aongus were resting in a hut. He could see a fire blazing, and smell the aroma of roasted wild boar. Gráinne rushed to greet Diarmaid, flinging her arms around him. Impulsively, he hugged her back. He realised now that he was beginning to fall in love with her.

They sat at the fire and ate their fill, and Diarmaid told Gráinne and Aongus how he had escaped from Fionn. They slept soundly that night, secure in the knowledge that, for a while at any rate, they were safe from their pursuers.

chapter five

The Warning

Aongus rose next morning at the crack of dawn.'I must leave you now,' he announced. 'But first, let me warn you: Do not go into a tree with only one trunk, or into a cave with only one opening or on to an island with only one way out.'

He paused and raised a warning finger. 'Wherever you cook your food, do not eat it in that place. And, wherever you eat, do not sleep in that same place. And, wherever you sleep one night, do not sleep there again another night.' Then Aongus left the hut and, spreading his cloak wide, flew back to the east.

Diarmaid and Gráinne too left the hut shortly afterwards and headed further westward until they came to a river. They were hungry and Diarmaid caught a salmon and built a fire to cook it on. Then, remembering Aongus's advice, the pair crossed the river and ate the salmon on the other bank. On they hurried, westward again, until it was dark. They rested that night in the shelter of a clump of trees.

Next morning they journeyed even further west. After

many miles of travel they were exhausted and sat down to rest.

Suddenly a tall young man emerged from a nearby wood and strode towards them. Diarmaid leapt to his feet and placed his hand on his sword.

'Do not be alarmed, Diarmaid,' the man said. 'My name is Muadhan, and Aongus has sent me to help you.'

'In what way?' Diarmaid enquired.

'I can help you in your travels during the day and keep watch for you at night.'

Diarmaid hesitated, unsure about trusting this stranger. He glanced questioningly at Gráinne.

'He has an honest face,' she whispered. 'And he is young and strong. Let him come with us.'

Diarmaid nodded and the three of them set off together. After a while they came to a broad river with a fast-flowing current. 'This river will be difficult to cross,' Diarmaid said.

'I will carry you both over on my shoulders,' Muadhan declared.

Diarmaid stared at him doubtfully. 'We will be too heavy for you,' he said.

Muadhan smiled, placed them both on his shoulders and carried them across the river. At the next river he did the same.

By now it was getting dark and Diarmaid and Gráinne were anxious to find a safe place to rest for the night. Muadhan guided them to a shallow cave, halfway up a mountain, which overlooked the sea. He spread soft rushes on the floor and hurried out of the cave.

At the foot of the mountain was a wood. Muadhan disappeared into the wood and cut a hazel rod. He tied a line and hook to the rod and stuck a holly berry on the hook. Then he went down to the sea and started to fish. Soon three fine fish lay on the rock beside him. He cooked the fish over a fire. The he hurried back to the cave with the roasting meal.

When they had eaten their fill Diarmaid and Gráinne remembered what Aongus had advised. They found another cave nearby and lay down on the rushes to sleep, while Muadhan sat outside and kept watch.

Next day, Gráinne kept watch while Muadhan slept in the cave, tired out after his night-long vigil. Diarmaid had left early to hunt in the hills nearby where boar and deer were plentiful. At mid-day, he stood on a hilltop gazing out to sea when a fleet of ships sailing into the bay below caught his attention. Three bearded men came ashore, followed by a crowd of fierce-looking warriors with long spears that glistened in the sun. The men saw Diarmaid and hurried up the hill towards him. He saluted them and asked them where they were from.

'We are three sea-kings from Scotland,' one of them said. 'Fionn Mac Cumhaill sent for us to track down an outlaw called Diarmaid Ó Duibhne. We have three blood-hounds with us to help us find him and neither fire nor water can stop them catching their quarry once they are set loose.'

Diarmaid pointed to the east. 'I saw the man you want

travelling in that direction yesterday,' he said. The sea-kings thanked him and returned to their ships to fetch their blood-hounds.

Meanwhile, Diarmaid raced back to the cave and told Gráinne and Muadhan what had happened. They left the cave and travelled swiftly further into the west. When Diarmaid and Gráinne grew tired, they stopped to rest. But Muadhan picked them up and carried them on his shoulder.

The three sea-kings returned and unleashed their blood-hounds. The dogs picked up the scent straightaway and, baying furiously, raced off in pursuit of the three runaways.

Diarmaid, Gráinne and Muadhan had stopped for a brief rest when they heard the howling of the blood-hounds. One hound drew ahead of the others and with snapping fangs ran towards Diarmaid.

Muadhan jumped up and took a small black pup from his tunic. He placed the pup on the ground and gave it an order. The pup launched itself at the hound, fastened its teeth in the big dog's throat and brought it crashing to the ground. It lay there without moving. The pup ran back to Muadhan, but one of the foreign warriors threw a spear which thudded into its neck and killed it.

Muadhan gave a little groan and motioned to the others to run. They raced away as fast as they could, but a second blood-hound soon caught up with them. Diarmaid turned to face the ferocious animal just as it leapt at him savagely. He raised a spear and drove it straight into the animal's eye. The hound dropped dead at his feet. Again, the three of them took to their heels. But they were forced to stop when they came to the edge of a steep precipice. The blood-thirsty baying of the third hound sounded closer and closer.

The hound bounded towards them, ready to tear them apart. The sea-kings and their warriors followed closely behind.

As the hound reached Diarmaid it leapt high in the air, its fangs stretched out for his throat. He ducked under the animal, caught it by its hind legs and, swinging it around, dashed its skull against a rock.

Then he flung the dead animal away and took up his spears. He sent three of them whizzing through the air in the direction of the approaching kings. Each king collapsed to the ground with a spear in his heart.

As for the warriors, when they saw their leaders being killed they turned on their heels and fled back to the ships.

Diarmaid, Gráinne and Muadhan rested that night in a wood by a river. Next morning Muadhan announced that he must leave them.

'Stay with us,' Diarmaid urged.

'I cannot,' replied Muadhan. 'Aongus told me to return after three days. I must obey his orders.'

He raised his hand in farewell and turned towards the east. Diarmaid and Gráinne turned in the opposite direction and journeyed swiftly on until they came to the great forest of Dubhrus which was guarded by a giant called Searbhan.

'We must be very careful,' Diarmaid warned. 'The guardian of this forest is a very bad-tempered giant and we must avoid upsetting him.'

With anxious eyes they made their way through the trees.

CHAPTER SIX

The Magic Quicken Tree

In the centre of the dark forest stood a magic quicken tree. It had not always been in the forest but came to be there because of a game of hurling held many years before between the Fianna and the Tuatha de Danann.

For food during the journey to and from the game the magical race of the Tuatha de Danann had brought from their home in the Land of Promise a supply of crimson nuts and arbutus apples and sweet quicken berries. These were magic foods, so the Tuatha de Danann took care that none of them should fall to the ground in Ireland. But as they passed through the Forest of Dubhrus one quicken berry fell to the ground.

A mighty quicken tree grew from that berry. So full of magic was it that anyone who ate one of its berries would never fall ill and the most ancient man or woman would immediately be young again if they swallowed three berries from the tree.

When the Tuatha de Danann found out that a quicken berry had taken root in Ireland, they sent Searbhan, one of their warriors, to guard the tree. Searbhan was a huge ugly giant with only one eye. No weapon could wound him, no fire could burn him and no water could drown him. The only way he could be killed was by three blows of his own club. Searbhan sat all day at the foot of the tree, keeping watch. At night he slept up in the highest branches. He allowed only one person to hunt in the forest on condition that he did not eat a single berry from the tree. That person was Diarmaid Ó Duibhne. But Diarmaid always took great care not to upset the bad-tempered giant.

Now, as Diarmaid built a hut for Gráinne and himself, he tried to make as little noise as possible.

Fionn, meantime, had returned to his fort on the Hill of Allen. But he had not given up hope of catching Diarmaid and Gráinne. One day two young warriors arrived at the fort and introduced themselves as Aongus, the son of Art Mac Morna, and Aodh, the son of Andala Mac Morna.

'I remember your fathers,' Fionn said in an icy voice. 'They fought against my father in the battle of Cnucha and killed him. And I outlawed you, their sons. So why have you disobeyed that order by coming here?'

'To make peace with you and to ask for our fathers' places in the ranks of the Fianna,' Aodh said.

Fionn's face grew red with rage. He opened his mouth to order their exile, when suddenly a plan occurred to him. 'I will let you have those places in the Fianna if you pay an *eiric*-fine for the death of my father,' he said quietly.

'What death-fine do you wish us to pay?' asked Aongus.

'The head of Diarmaid Ó Duibhne or a handful of berries from the magic quicken tree in the Forest of Dubhrus,' Fionn replied.

Oisín, who was standing beside his father, shook his head. 'Take my advice, go away and forget about this,' he said to the warriors. 'Otherwise you will lose your lives in trying to pay that fine.'

'We would rather die than go back now,' Aodh said.

He looked at Fionn. 'We will do our best to bring you Diarmaid's head or the magic berries.'

And they hurried away, clutching their weapons. After several days' travel they came to the hut in the Forest of Dubhrus where Diarmaid and Gráinne were hiding. When Diarmaid heard them approaching he snatched up his spear and ran out.

'Who are you?' he demanded.

The warriors told him their names.

'Why have you come here?'

'We owe Fionn Mac Cumhaill a death-fine for his father. It must be paid by our bringing him the head of Diarmaid Ó Duibhne or a handful of berries from the magic quicken tree. Perhaps you can tell us where to find Diarmaid?'

'I am the man you seek,' Diarmaid said with a grim smile on his lips. 'But I have no intention of parting with my head. And I doubt if you can get the berries either for you must first fight Searbhan the Giant for them. No weapon can wound him, no fire can burn him and no water can drown him.' Diarmaid paused and raised his spear. 'Do you want to try for my head first?'

'Yes,' Aodh said. 'But let us put aside our weapons and fight with our bare hands. If we win we will cut off your head and take it back to Fionn. If you win you can cut off our heads and hang them up in your hut.'

Diarmaid nodded in agreement and the fight began. But the warriors were no match for Diarmaid who threw them to the ground and tied their hands and feet. Then he took out his sword and held it over their heads.

'Wait!' Gráinne cried out. 'I have a great longing for some berries from that quicken tree. Three of you would have a better chance of defeating the giant and getting me the berries.'

'The giant could kill the three of us if we try to steal those berries,' Diarmaid said.

'Has the brave Diarmaid Ó Duibhne turned coward?' Gráinne taunted him.

'Never,' Diarmaid said.

'Go and fetch the berries then.'

'Let us go with you,' the two warriors pleaded.

Diarmaid hesitated and then untied them. They followed him as he set off for the quicken tree where the giant was dozing after a huge meal. Diarmaid prodded him with his foot and woke him up.

Searbhan's big eye flickered open. He glared at Diarmaid. 'What do you want?'

'Gráinne has a longing for some berries from that tree

you are guarding,' Diarmaid said. 'I have come to take a handful of them.'

'I will not let you take one berry even if it were to save her life!' the giant snarled.

'I must have them one way or the other,' Diarmaid declared.

With an angry bellow the giant sprang to his feet, raised his club over his head, and rained three mighty blows down on Diarmaid. But Diarmaid's shield took the force of the blows, shattering it into pieces. Diarmaid then jumped in underneath Searbhan's guard and tripped the giant, sending him crashing to the ground.

Then he quickly grabbed the giant's club where it lay on the ground and struck Searbhan three blows on the head. The giant groaned and stretched out dead.

The two warriors ran over and stared down at the giant's body.

'Bury the giant,' he ordered. 'Then go and bring Gráinne here.' And he sank on to his knees, exhausted by the fight.

When Gráinne arrived, Diarmaid rose and picked a handful of berries from the tree. He gave her the berries and kept on picking more until she had eaten her fill. Then he gave a bunch of berries to the warriors of Morna.

'Take these to Fionn,' he said, 'and tell him it was you who killed Searbhan the Giant.'

They thanked him and set off for Fionn's fort. 'We have killed Searbhan the Giant,' they told the Fianna leader.

'Prove it,' said Fionn.

Aodh handed him the berries. 'These are from the magic quicken tree and we have brought them to you in payment of the death-fine for your father.'

Fionn took the berries and smelled them. 'It was Diarmaid Ó Duibhne who took these berries, not you!' he snapped. 'I smell his touch on them. It was he and not you who killed that giant. Now that I know where he is I shall catch him unawares and kill him!'

CHAPTER SEVEN

Trapped in the Tree

Fionn marched with all his warriors to the forest of Dubhrus. On the edge of the forest the trackers picked up the trail of Diarmaid and Gráinne and arrived at the magic quicken tree. High up in the tree-tops, in the giant's house, Diarmaid and Gráinne watched Fionn as he yawned and sat down at the foot of the tree.

'The day is hot and I will rest here for a while,' he said. 'I know that Diarmaid and Gráinne are hiding up in the tree. But they cannot escape as long as we keep the tree surrounded.'

Oisín shook his head doubtfully. 'I don't think Diarmaid has remained in this tree while you have been trailing him,' he declared.

Fionn shrugged. 'We shall see,' and he called for a chessboard to be brought to him. 'I'll play a game with you, Oisín,' he said.

Soon Oisín was close to defeat.

'You have one move left, Oisín,' warned Fionn. 'It could win or lose this game for you.' He frowned at the watching circle of warriors. 'Let no one tell him what that move should be.'

Oisín stared at the chessboard, unable to decide on the right move. From their hiding-place in the branches above, Diarmaid and Gráinne watched. 'I'd like to help Oisín,' Diarmaid whispered.

'Do not!' Gráinne cautioned. 'There are hundreds of warriors down there waiting to kill you.'

'Oisín has often helped me,' he said. 'Why shouldn't I help him now?'

And before Gráinne could stop him, Diarmaid had plucked a magic berry from the tree and tossed it down on top of one of Oisín's chesspieces. The berry rolled from there on to another square on the board. Oisín moved the piece to that square and won the game.

He and Fionn played another game. Soon Oisín was just one move away from winning or losing. Again, Diarmaid dropped a magic berry on top of a chesspiece and it bounced onto a square on the board. Oisín moved the piece to that square and won the game.

Fionn was beginning to get angry. They played a third time. The same thing happened again and Oisín won that game also. This time Fionn glared across the board at him.

'It is no wonder you are able to win with Diarmaid Ó Duibhne, the best chess-player in Ireland, helping you,' he growled.

Oisín's son, Oscar, shook his head. 'Why would Diarmaid do a thing like that when he knows that you are pursuing him?'

Trapped in the Tree

Fionn stared up at the tree. 'Which of us is right, Diarmaid?'

Now Diarmaid was honour-bound to answer his old captain's question, and he replied, 'You are, Fionn Mac Cumhaill.'

As he spoke, Diarmaid saw the fear on Gráinne's face. He reached out, put his arms around her and kissed her. Fionn saw this through a gap in the branches and his face flushed with anger.

'You will pay for that kiss with your head, Diarmaid Ó Duibhne!' he bellowed. He ordered his warriors to gather in circles under the tree, linking their hands together so that nobody could get through. Then he offered his armour and weapons and a very high place in the Fianna to any man who would climb the tree and bring back Diarmaid's head.

The warrior Garbh of Slieve Cua shouted, 'I will do it! Diarmaid's father killed my father and I will seek vengeance!' And he began to climb the tree.

Far away in his cave at Brú na Boinne, Aongus again had a sudden feeling that all was not well with his foster-son. He looked into the water in his magic bowl and immediately saw the danger surrounding Diarmaid and Gráinne. He went to the mouth of the cave, spread wide his cloak, and flew swiftly on the wind westwards. The topmost branches of the quicken tree shook slightly as Aongus alighted but Fionn and his warriors down below saw nothing because his magic cloak shielded him from their gaze.

Garbh climbed carefully up the tree. When he came close to Diarmaid he drew his sword and swung it through the air. Diarmaid avoided the blow and, with a swift kick, sent Garbh crashing through leaves and branches to the ground. As the warrior fell, Aongus whispered a spell which transformed Garbh into the double of Diarmaid and, when he landed on the ground, one of the Fianna ran forward and chopped off his head.

Garbh's body immediately assumed its true likeness and Fionn and his warriors were furious when they saw it was their comrade they had been tricked into killing.

Other warriors rushed to climb the tree and try to cut off Diarmaid's head. But each warrior received the same treatment. Soon nine headless bodies lay at the foot of the quicken tree.

Fionn seethed with anger. 'You will not escape me despite your tricks, Diarmaid Ó Duibhne!' he shouted up at the tree.

Gráinne glanced anxiously at Diarmaid. 'What will we do now? You cannot fight them all.'

Diarmaid shook his head in doubt. 'Do not worry,' Aongus said. 'I will take you with me under my cloak to my cave at Brú na Boinne. You will be safe there.'

Diarmaid shook his head. 'Take Gráinne with you,' he said. 'I will stay here and try to fight my way out. If I succeed I will follow you. If not, bring Gráinne back to her father at Tara.'

'No! I will stay here and fight by your side,' Gráinne declared. 'Give me a weapon.'

Diarmaid kissed her gently. 'Go, my love. I would die now if any harm came to you.'

Aongus put his cloak over Gráinne and, unseen by the warriors below, flew with her on the wind to Brú na Boinne.

When they had gone Diarmaid took his weapons in his hands and prepared for the hardest fight of his life.

chapter eight

The Escape

Diarmaid looked down at Fionn from his perch in the quicken tree. Then in a loud clear voice he declared, 'I am coming down from this tree now, and I shall kill as many of you as I can because I know you will never forgive me but will always seek my death instead.'

He paused and gazed at the upturned faces. 'But remember this,' he continued. 'Never was the Fianna in danger that I did not share that danger with you. And never was there a battle that I did not go into first for your sake, and come out of it last. But now I have no choice but to fight you all and make you pay dearly for my life.'

There was silence for a moment. Then Oscar went over to Fionn. 'What Diarmaid says is true. He has always fought bravely for us. Forgive him.'

'Never!' Fionn yelled. 'He shall have peace and forgiveness only when he is dead.'

'Then I take his protection upon myself,' Oscar said gravely. 'And if any man should harm Diarmaid while he is under my protection may the earth open and swallow him and may the sky and the stars fall upon my head.'

He stared up into the tree. 'Come down, Diarmaid!' he shouted. 'I will defend you against any treachery.'

But Diarmaid shook his head and climbing out on a springy branch of the tree he stretched up as tall as he could for a second. Then, with a huge jump, he flew like a bird up from the branch and out over Fionn and the warriors below, until he came to rest on the grass at the edge of the forest. Oscar raced after him and together they hurried away to Brú na Boinne where they were given a warm welcome by Aongus and Gráinne.

Fionn realised now that he would have to try some other plan to get the better of Diarmaid. He returned to his fort and gave orders for his best ship to be made ready and provisioned for a journey.

When the ship was ready, Fionn boarded it with a hundred of his warriors and they set sail. The ship glided out to sea and skimmed over the waves until it reached the shores of Scotland. Fionn leapt ashore and, with five of his warriors, went to see the King of Scotland who was an old friend.

The king had a feast prepared in his honour. When they had eaten and drunk their fill Fionn turned to the king and told him how Diarmaid Ó Duibhne had wronged him by running away with Gráinne.

'I want you to help me find him so that I can punish him,' he said. 'Give me as many of your warriors as you can spare and this will make it easier for me to track him down.'

The king nodded his head. 'I too would like to see Diarmaid Ó Duibhne dead. He killed my brothers in combat when he visited this country some years ago.' He thumped the table with his fist. 'I will give you my two sons and a thousand warriors to help you track him down and slay him.'

Fionn thanked the king and, feeling in better spirits now, returned to the ship. When they came within sight of Ireland again, Fionn ordered the ship to be anchored in an inlet near Brú na Boinne. He knew Aongus was Diarmaid's foster-father and suspected that he was sheltering Gráinne and his foster-son. Then he sent a messenger to Aongus's cave with a challenge to Diarmaid to come out and do battle with him and his warriors.

Diarmaid was under *geasa* never to refuse a challenge to combat. So, despite the pleadings of Gráinne, he put on his armour and prepared to go out and fight. Oscar also donned his armour and both young men fastened their shields together so that they could not be separated in the battle.

The sons of the King of Scotland, accompanied by their warriors, were first into combat. With swift slashes of their swords Diarmaid and Oscar carved their way through their ranks like hungry wolves attacking a flock of sheep.

By nightfall the Scottish princes and their men lay dead on the battle-field and Diarmaid and Oscar returned unharmed to join Aongus and Gráinne in the cave.

Fionn watched the terrible slaughter from his ship. He had intended to attack with his own warriors the following morning but he knew now that something besides force was necessary to overcome Diarmaid. He barked an order. The ship was to set sail for the Land of Promise where the witch who was his foster-mother lived.

'No warrior or army can defeat Diarmaid Ó Duibhne in battle,' Fionn said to his foster-mother. 'Witchcraft is the only way to get the better of him.'

The witch's eyes glittered with venom. 'Any enemy of yours is an enemy of mine!' she hissed. 'I shall go with you to Ireland and use my magic to kill this man!'

They sailed back to Ireland and into the inlet near Brú na Boinne. The witch threw a magic mist over the ship so that no one would know Fionn and his warriors were there.

Oscar had said goodbye to Diarmaid and Gráinne the previous day, thinking that his friends were now safe. Today Diarmaid was out hunting and the witch was aware of this. She went ashore and, picking up a water-lily leaf, she turned it into a millstone with a hole in the centre. Seating herself on the millstone, she rose into the air and floated on a magic wind until she was directly over Diarmaid.

Ping! The witch shot little poisoned darts at him through the hole in the millstone. The darts pierced his armour and clothes, burning him with a terrible venom that he could not shake off no matter which way he twisted or turned. He realised that he was doomed to die unless he could kill the witch quickly.

Lying on his back Diarmaid raised the *ga dearg*, his most deadly spear, and launched it at the hole in the millstone. The spear shot through the hole and went straight into the witch's body. With an agonised cry she fell dead to the ground.

Grabbing her hair, Diarmaid cut off her head and brought it back to Brú na Boinne.

'Will Fionn never stop pursuing us?' Gráinne groaned, when she saw Diarmaid clutching the witch's severed head.

'Never,' came Diarmaid's solemn reply.

Aongus stared at them thoughtfully. 'I wonder,' he said. 'The death of the witch may have given him food for thought. I think I shall go and see Fionn Mac Cumhaill tomorrow.'

ChAPTER NINE

Peace

Next morning Aongus left the cave and hurried down to where Fionn's ship was anchored in the inlet near Brú na Boinne. Since the death of the witch the ship was no longer hidden in a magic mist. Fionn knew now that no force or magic he was aware of could help him kill Diarmaid. He was about to give orders for the ship to sail away when Aongus approached and said he wished to talk to him. Reluctantly Fionn allowed him to come on board.

'What does the foster-father of my greatest enemy wish to talk to me about?' Fionn demanded icily.

'Peace,' Aongus responded. 'There is no point in continuing this feud with Diarmaid. Some of your best warriors have already died. More will die if this continues. All it has brought is misery and death. Are you prepared to make peace with him?'

Fionn hesitated. Then slowly he nodded his head.

'Good!' Aongus smiled. 'Now I must go and talk with the High King.'

He went quickly to Tara and sought an audience with

Cormac. He explained that Fionn was willing to make peace with Diarmaid.

'Will you pardon Diarmaid for running away with your daughter?' he asked.

The king tugged thoughtfully at his beard. 'Yes,' he said, provided my son, Cairbre, who will be king after me, also agrees.'

So Aongus talked to Cairbre who smiled and said, 'I never wished to see Gráinne married to Fionn Mac Cumhaill. I would prefer her to have Diarmaid as her husband. He has never been my enemy so there is nothing for me to forgive.'

Aongus returned to the cave and told Diarmaid all that had happened. 'Are you willing to make peace now with Fionn and Cormac?' he asked.

'Yes,' Diarmaid replied, 'on certain conditions.'

'What are they?'

'I want the lands in Munster that were my father's given back to me. They must be free of any tribute to the High King. Neither Fionn nor the Fianna shall be allowed to go hunting on them. Also, I want Fionn to give me the lands of Beann Damhais in Leinster.'

'I will ask Fionn and Cormac if they agree with those terms,' Aongus said.

He hurried back to Fionn and the High King and, after some hesitation on their part and some persuasion on the part of Aongus, they agreed to Diarmaid's conditions.

So peace was made at last and Diarmaid and Gráinne

built a grand house at Rath Gráinne on the lands of Ceis Corann and went to live there. They had five sons and one daughter and they prospered and grew very rich.

But their troubles were not over yet.

CHAPTER TEN

The Geis

The happy and peaceful years went by. Then, one day, as they were walking in the garden, Gráinne said to Diarmaid, 'We have vast lands and many herds. We have a magnificent house and dozens of servants. And yet we have never entertained beneath our roof the greatest man in Ireland – the greatest man that is, apart from my father, the High King Fionn Mac Cumhaill, Captain of the Fianna.'

Diarmaid said nothing for a long time. Then he replied, 'You know why I have never invited Fionn here. Although there is peace between us we are not friends.'

'If we invite him and the chief warriors of the Fianna to a great feast he may become our friend again,' Gráinne said. 'I would prefer him as a friend than an enemy.'

Again Diarmaid was silent.

'Well?' Gráinne enquired at last. 'What do you think?'

'I suppose it can do no harm,' Diarmaid replied.

So a great feast was prepared in Rath Gráinne and Fionn and his chief warriors were invited. After the feast they spent many days as guests at Rath Gráinne. Diarmaid even gave them permission to hunt on his lands. But there was one animal no one was allowed to hunt – the wild boar – for Diarmaid was under a *geis* never to hunt a boar.

This had come about because of something that had happened many years before when Diarmaid was being fostered by Aongus at Brú na Boinne. At that time Aongus also fostered a son of his steward, who was Diarmaid's half-brother, so that Diarmaid would have a companion to play with.

One day Diarmaid's father, Donn Ó Duibhne, came to visit to see how his son was getting on. That evening a fierce fight broke out between two hounds. As the servants tried to pull the dogs apart, the steward's son ran for shelter between Donn's knees. Donn felt a sudden surge of hatred for this boy who was the result of his wife's infidelity and closed his knees so tightly that he killed the child on the spot. Then, in an effort to cover his crime, he flung the child's body under the feet of the fighting hounds.

When the hounds were parted the steward found his son's body. He picked it up and in an anguished voice he shouted, 'The hounds have killed my son!'

But the man who owned the hounds pointed out that no bite or scratch could be found on the child's body. The only marks were those on his crushed sides.

The steward guessed then what had happened. He demanded that the child Diarmaid should be placed between his knees to be crushed the way his son had been.

Donn jumped angrily to his feet and would have cut

the steward's head off had Aongus not come between them. The steward hurried from the hall and returned with Aongus's magic wand. He touched his son's body with the wand and it was changed immediately into a wild black boar with neither ears nor tail.

'I put this spell on you,' the steward chanted over the boar, 'that I put as well on Diarmaid. You shall both have the same span of life and when Diarmaid dies you shall be the cause of his death!'

The boar ran out of the hall and disappeared into the night. Aongus was very worried. How could Diarmaid escape the death-spell that the steward had put on him? He decided to place a *geis* on his foster-child never to hunt wild boar.

And that was the reason why, during the stay of Fionn and the Fianna at Rath Gráinne, they were allowed to hunt any wild animal except boars.

One night while Fionn and his warriors were still at Rath Gráinne, Diarmaid woke suddenly from his sleep and sat up in bed.

'What's the matter?' Gráinne asked, waking too.

'I heard a hound baying as if out on a hunt,' he replied. 'It is a strange sound to hear in the middle of the night.'

'It was probably one of the Tuatha de Danann's magic hounds,' Gráinne said. 'They often go hunting at night. Now lie down and go back to sleep.'

Diarmaid went to sleep once more. But he woke when

he heard the baying of the hound echoing through the night again. He rose and dressed and was about to go out to see what the noise was about, but Gráinne persuaded him to go back to bed. Once more he got back into bed and once more he was woken by the loud baying of the hound.

Daylight was now beginning to filter in through the window, and Diarmaid rose and put on his cloak.

'I shall go and find out what hound is causing that noise,' he said. 'It cannot be one of the Tuatha de Danann's hounds for they do not go hunting after sunrise. Perhaps it is one of our own hounds that has strayed and got lost.'

A feeling of fear gripped Gráinne. 'Take the *ga dearg*, your best spear, with you,' she pleaded. 'You will need it if you run into any danger.'

Diarmaid shook his head. 'What danger can come from a lost hound?' he smiled.

'Well, take some weapon with you.'

'I will take the *ga bui*, my light spear, as well as my faithful hound, Mac an Chuill.'

He placed a collar and chain on Mac an Chuill and set off in the direction from which the baying had come. As he drew near Ben Bulben he heard the sound again, together with the baying of other hounds, as though a whole pack was out hunting.

Diarmaid climbed to the top of Ben Bulben. There he was surprised to find Fionn Mac Cumhaill standing alone.

'Is it you who is hunting here?' Diarmaid demanded.

'No,' Fionn replied. 'Some of my men took the hounds out during the night. One of the hounds found the scent of a wild boar and the others followed him. I would have stopped them if I could but I was too late.'

He frowned. 'The trail they follow is that of the Wild Boar of Ben Bulben. But they are wasting their time chasing it, for it cannot be caught. It has killed many men and hounds over the years.'

He stared over Diarmaid's shoulder and his eyes widened. 'Look! The boar is heading this way now. My men are running from it.'

Diarmaid twirled around and saw the boar rushing up the hill towards them.

'We must get out of its way!' Fionn urged.

'I will not run away from any animal,' Diarmaid declared.

'Do not stand and fight it,' Fionn advised. 'Remember you are under a *geis* never to hunt a wild boar.'

'No matter. I will stand my ground now.'

'Very well, then.' Fionn shrugged and walked away, leaving Diarmaid to face the wild boar alone.

But Diarmaid noticed a sly smile steal over Fionn's face as he turned away. 'I wonder if Fionn started this chase deliberately so as to bring about my death?' he mused. He sighed deeply. 'Well, if I am fated to die here what can I do about it?'

And Diarmaid prepared to face the wild boar as it came charging towards him up the hill.

CHAPTER ELEVEN

The Treachery of
Fionn Mac Cumhaill

The great boar thundered closer and closer. Diarmaid loosed his hound Mac an Chuill against it. But the hound turned and ran from the fierce razor-tusked boar.

Diarmaid's heart sank. 'I should have taken Gráinne's advice and brought the *ga dearg* with me,' he murmured. 'Now I shall have to do the best I can with these weapons.'

He slipped his finger into the silken loop of the *ga buí* and hurled the spear at the boar, striking it in the centre of its forehead. But the weapon failed to disturb even a bristle on the charging animal.

Still the boar closed in. Diarmaid drew his sword and crashed it down with all his might on the animal's wide black back. Again, not a bristle on the boar moved, but the sword broke into two pieces. Then the animal caught Diarmaid a furious blow with his tusks that flung him high in the air.

He landed across the boar's back and off it charged,

down the slope, carrying Diarmaid along on its back. It ran so swiftly that Diarmaid had no chance to scramble down to the ground.

Then, at the foot of the mountain, the boar stopped suddenly in its tracks. Diarmaid shot straight over its head and landed right in front of the animal. With a furious bellow it gored him savagely with its tusks, slashing a gaping wound in his side.

The boar turned to gore Diarmaid again but, with what remained of his ebbing strength, he thrust the remnant of the sword still in his hand into the boar's soft flank, penetrating its heart. The Wild Boar of Ben Bulben rolled over dead on its back.

Fionn and the rest of the hunting party heard the commotion and they ran down to see what had happened. Diarmaid was lying on the ground trying desperately to hold onto life as blood pumped from the wound in his side.

Fionn went over and stared down at him. 'It pleases me to see you like this, Diarmaid,' he gloated. 'Your days of heroism in battle and gallantry in love will soon be ended.'

'Not if you cure me,' Diarmaid gasped.

'How?' Fionn asked.

'You took the Salmon of Knowledge from the River Boyne and a drink of water from your cupped hands will heal even a dying man.'

'Why should I save your life?'

'Because I often saved yours,' Diarmaid groaned with

pain. Then, through gritted teeth, he added, 'Don't you remember the time we went to the house of Deirg Mac Dolair to enjoy a feast and while we were sitting around the table, Cairbre, your enemy, and the men of Tara and Meath, came and surrounded the place and set the roof on fire.'

Diarmaid groaned again and drew a deep breath to give him the strength to continue. 'I sallied forth myself,' he continued, 'and quenched the fire. Then I turned on your enemies, killed half of them and put the rest to flight. When I returned to the feasting hall you greeted me with open arms. If I had asked you for a drink from your cupped hands that night you would have given it to me gladly.'

'That time maybe, but not now,' said Fionn, 'for since then you have betrayed me by stealing Gráinne from me at Tara, even though you were my trusted friend that night.'

'It was not my fault,' Diarmaid whispered. 'Gráinne laid a *geis* on me and you know well that I cannot break a spell like that when it is put on me.'

'I don't believe you!' Fionn snapped.

Diarmaid sighed. 'Remember the night the treacherous Miodhach Mac Colgain invited you to a feast in the Hostel of the Quicken Trees. And he had plotted with three kings from the Underworld to cut off your head. You did not know and went with some of the Fianna to the feast … Remember?'

Fionn nodded curtly.

'During the night Miodhach played a magic trick on you so that you and your men were stuck tightly to the ground. Then he slipped away to summon the three kings to come and kill you. But you managed to put your thumb under your tooth of knowledge and you discovered the treachery that was planned. So you sent a thought-message to me asking for help ...'

Diarmaid paused and gasped for breath once more, before carrying on. 'And I hurried at once to your rescue,' he said. 'And I defended the ford leading to the hostel so as to prevent your enemies attacking you while you lay there helpless. Then I killed the three kings and brought their heads back on my shield to the hostel. I sprinkled their blood beneath you and your men and you were immediately set free.'

With a great effort, Diarmaid raised his head and stared into Fionn's eyes. 'Remember?'

'Yes.'

'If I had asked you for a drink that night you would not have refused me.'

'Not that night,' Fionn said. 'But now ...' He shook his head.

'Yes, even now!' Diarmaid reached out weakly and touched Fionn's arm. 'Give me a drink from your hands,' he pleaded. 'I feel death approaching.'

Fionn slowly shook his head again. Diarmaid sighed and slumped back on the ground. Oscar came forward and knelt down by his friend, cradling Diarmaid's head on his knee. He glanced up angrily at Fionn.

'Give him a drink from your cupped hands before it is too late!' he urged.

'There is no water to be had around here,' Fionn declared.

'That is not true,' Diarmaid whispered. 'There is a spring of lovely clear water only nine paces from this place.'

Fionn looked around at the accusing eyes of his companions. Then, very reluctantly, he turned and went to the spring. He cupped his hands and filled them with water and turned to bring it back to Diarmaid, but on the way he thought bitterly once more of how Diarmaid had run away with Gráinne. Opening his fingers, he let the water trickle down to the ground.

'It slipped through my fingers,' he said to the others.

'You did that deliberately!' Oscar said angrily. 'Go back and try again.'

So Fionn went over to the spring once more and filled his cupped hands with water. Again, on the way back, he thought of Gráinne and again he let the water trickle from his hands.

'If you do not bring the water this third time only one of us shall leave this place alive!' Oscar swore.

Fionn went once more to the spring and, cupping his hands, filled them with water. But this time he did not spill any of it on the way back for he had no wish to engage his grandson in mortal combat.

But at the very moment that he knelt down by Diarmaid's body the wounded warrior heaved a great sigh and died.

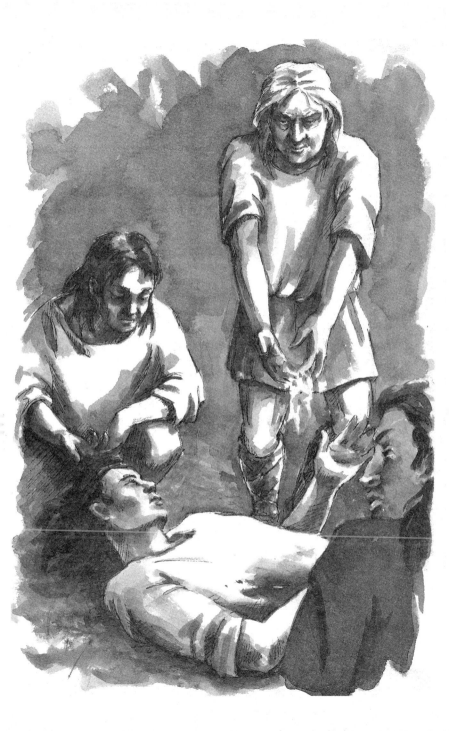

The Fianna gathered around Diarmaid's body and gave three loud cries of mourning for his death. Then Oscar laid Diarmaid's head gently on the ground and leapt angrily to his feet. Glaring at Fionn he shouted, 'You deserve to have your head cut off!'

His hand gripped his sword tightly, but Oisín moved in between his son and Fionn.

'One tragedy is enough for today,' he said. 'Let us go now before Aongus arrives and thinks that all of us were responsible for his foster-son's death.'

So the Fianna went away, with Fionn holding the leash of Diarmaid's hound, Mac an Chuill. But Oscar and Oisín and two other friends of Diarmaid's slipped back and placed their cloaks over his body before following Fionn and the others back to Gráinne's house.

Gráinne was watching anxiously for Diarmaid's return. When she saw the group of Fianna approaching with Fionn at their head leading Diarmaid's hound, she knew that something terrible had happened to her husband. A long keening cry burst from her throat and she fell unconscious to the ground.

Later, when she recovered consciousness, Fionn told Gráinne how Diarmaid had died. She ordered her servants to go to Ben Bulben and bring home his body. Turning angrily to Fionn, she said, 'Go away now but leave me Diarmaid's hound.'

'I wish to keep it,' Fionn said in a surly voice. 'It is a good hunting hound and it is no use to you.'

Gráinne stared at him with hatred smouldering in her

eyes. Then Oisín came forward and, taking the hound's leash from Fionn, he handed it to Gráinne. 'Let us leave Diarmaid's wife to her grief,' he said.

He turned and set off for the fort on the Hill of Allen, followed by Fionn and the rest of the Fianna.

When Gráinne's people arrived at Ben Bulben they found Aongus standing sadly over Diarmaid's body. Behind him stood three hundred of his Tuatha de Danann warriors. Gráinne's servants hesitated when they saw them but the warriors turned out the back of their shields as a sign of peace and the servants approached the body.

Then both groups gave three great cries of keening in lament for Diarmaid. Aongus asked Gráinne's people why they had come there.

'Princess Gráinne sent us to bring home Diarmaid's body,' the chief servant said.

Aongus shook his head firmly. 'No, that would not be proper now,' he said. 'It is on account of Gráinne that Diarmaid has died. I shall take his body back to my place at Brú na Boinne where he was fostered by me.'

He ordered Diarmaid's body to be placed on a golden bier with his spears fixed at each corner, points upwards. Then Aongus and his warriors walked in solemn procession to Brú na Boinne, carrying the funeral bier in turn on their shoulders.

And, until she died, Gráinne mourned the death by treachery of the only man she had ever truly loved.